Dracula

Dracula

STEPHANIE BAUDET

MADCAP

For Andrée Michele,
with Love

Published in Great Britain in 1999
by Madcap Books,
André Deutsch Ltd, 76 Dean Street, London W1V 5HA
www.vci.co.uk

Copyright © 1999 Stephanie Baudet

The right of Stephanie Baudet to be identified as the author of
this work has been asserted by her in accordance with the
Copyright, Designs and Patents Act, 1988

A catalogue record for this book is available from the British
Library

ISBN 0 233 99578 1

Typeset in Liverpool by Derek Doyle & Associates
Printed in Great Britain

Chapter 1

'It's getting foggy,' said Sarah. She skidded to a stop, almost crashing into me. 'I think we ought to go down by cable car.'

'It's low cloud,' I said, trying not to get irritated, 'not fog.'

'What's the difference? We can't see. It's getting thicker every minute. I hate skiing when I can't see where I'm going. Everything's white, you can't see the bumps and you can easily go off piste. Then you're in trouble.'

I sighed, pushed up my goggles and placed my ski pole in the depression on my ski bindings, ready to release them. Then I stopped. No! Why should I do what *she* wanted, especially on the last day of our holiday? This was the last ski run I'd get for a whole year. As it was, she'd ruined the holiday, she and her mother. I'd wanted to bring a friend who could ski properly but no, everything had changed. Dad had married again and suddenly I'd not only got a step-mother but a stepsister too. I hadn't asked for them and I didn't want them.

'I'm skiing down,' I said, putting on my goggles again. 'You can do what you want.' I dug in my poles and pushed off towards the red run, feeling annoyed, especially when I heard her following. Couldn't she do anything on her own? Did she *have* to do everything I did? I wanted to fly down the mountain and feel the wind in my hair and the snow prickle against my face – it was beginning to snow again. Now I'd have to look out for her as usual, act as baby minder, even though she was twelve, two years older than me.

I didn't speak to her. Well, you can't talk much when you're skiing anyway, only if you stop, and I wasn't going to do that. She would just have to keep up with me. And she did. I'll give her that. She'd only skied once before and we came every year. WE. Mum, Dad and me. That's what WE used to mean. Now it doesn't mean that any more. Now it means Dad, me and THEM. I don't even know what to call her mum. I can't call her Mrs Harker, can I, and I can't call her mum either. I've got a mum. I pointed my skis downhill and crouched down for the schuss. Straight down, faster and faster. Let her try and keep up with that. She was really proud of the ski badge she'd been given that morning, but I'd show her it didn't mean much.

I waited for her to call out for me to stop but she didn't. When I looked round she was there, right behind me, her pale hair all windswept round her face.

There were plenty of other people around so we just followed them, when we could see them. The fog was getting thicker. Then suddenly there was no one. We were alone on the slope and the snow was deeper and smooth. No one had skied here recently, if ever.

I stopped and she did too, taking off her sunglasses and looking at me as if to say 'I told you so'; her eyes were angry rather than afraid. At least she didn't start crying or anything. And I knew that she'd been right in the first place, though I wasn't going to admit it. We should have gone down in the cable car. Dad would be real mad and she wouldn't take any of the blame.

'We can't be far off piste,' I said. 'It must be over to the left somewhere. Look out for those red and white poles.'

We never saw any. Nothing but white all round. A white-out. Luckily the slope became flatter and then we reached what looked like a road, though it was well covered with snow and there were no tyre marks.

'We can't be far from the village,' said Sarah. I couldn't see the logic in that. Just because we'd found a road didn't mean we were near anywhere. This was Rumania. We'd never been here before and had only come this time because the skiing was cheaper.

'There's a sign,' said Sarah, skiing to it and dusting the snow off the top with her gloved hand. 'It says *Borgo Pass*.'

'That doesn't help much,' I said.

'Well I wasn't to know. It might have said *Vatra one mile*.'

'Kilometre.'

'Kilometre, then.'

A sudden mournful sound rose out of the darkness nearby and echoed round the rocky slopes. Then another and another. A sound that sent shivers down my spine. I'd never heard anything like it before, but I knew what it was.

Wolves.

At the same time there came another sound and we both looked up as a strange vehicle loomed out of the fog. It was a sleigh pulled by four coal-black horses. The driver was a tall man, his face partly hidden by a huge black hat, but despite that and the fog, as he slowed down I could still see his eyes, which seemed to gleam red like two small glowing embers.

'We're lost,' I said. 'Could you please tell us the way back to Vatra?' I knew that he probably didn't understand English so I repeated the name of our village.

He nodded and pointed to the sleigh.

'He's going to give us a lift,' said Sarah, already clicking open her ski bindings and taking off her skis.

We had hardly got them off and thrown them into the sleigh when the driver's hand stretched out and long fingers grasped Sarah and flung her into the carriage. The hand seemed to hesitate a moment before reaching towards me. I caught a glimpse of it in the light of the carriage lamp. The fingers had long sharp pointed nails, like knives. I cowered back. Well anyone would have. There was something wrong. Something unnatural about that hand. How could it stretch this far? How could it reach out and lift Sarah right off the ground when the coachman was still sitting up in his driving seat?

But Sarah was already inside. I couldn't leave her, even if I wanted to. Even if I wished she'd never come into my life.

The hand grasped my jacket, throwing me down onto the hard leather seat of the sleigh while the door slammed shut behind me. I heard a voice, then a face appeared briefly at the side of the sleigh and something was flung inside, clattering to the floor. There was the crack of a whip and we took off at breakneck speed as if the devil himself were after us.

Chapter 2

We clung tightly to the sides to stop ourselves from being thrown about the sleigh.

'Is he in a hurry or what?' asked Sarah. 'We can't be too far from the village.' She looked at me. I could just see the outline of her face and her ski hat in the dim light of the lamp.

'Jon? Did you see the way he. . . ?' She didn't finish the sentence. I knew what she meant. The way he'd practically flung us into the sleigh.

'At home we'd never accept a lift from a stranger,' she continued, 'but . . .'

'We were lost,' I said. 'Sometimes you have to trust people when you're in trouble.'

The sleigh slowed to a gentler pace and I thought we must be there by now but there was no sign of lights or houses. The wind was rising and howled and moaned round the rocks and through the swaying trees.

'I'm frozen,' said Sarah. We found a blanket under the seat and she came and sat next to me so that we could share it. Snow began to fall, softly at first, and then larger flakes swirled down dusting everything in glowing white. The sleigh's runners swished on a soft carpet of new snow, skidding a little from time to time.

At last the clouds cleared away and the moon came out over the jagged mountain tops revealing a wild countryside covered in a smooth white blanket. Wolves began to howl again, making the horses skitter about nervously until at last the driver was forced to stop.

I was really worried now. We'd gone miles. Where was he taking us?

Sarah half stood up. 'I'm getting out. Come on, Jon.'

'We can't. We have to go with him.'

'Why?' Her voice was getting shrill, like the rising wind. 'Why do we?'

'Because we'd freeze to death out here. Have you seen a single house along the way?'

She sank back on to the seat. We watched the driver standing in front of the horses, whispering soothingly, stroking their trembling necks until they quietened. Then he climbed back into his seat and we were off again.

After about twenty minutes we saw a building up ahead. It looked like a castle, with huge turrets and battlements forming a grim silhouette against the moonlit sky. No light shone from any window.

Sarah grabbed my arm. 'It's like something out of a horror movie,' she whispered, and I noted the shake in her voice. I was afraid to speak in case mine shook too.

The driver helped us out of the sleigh, and I winced at his iron grip. He pointed at the castle door and then flung our skis out into the snowy courtyard. We still had the blanket draped round our shoulders as we walked towards the stone porch and the great oak door.

'There doesn't seem to be a bell or knocker,' I said, searching with my fingers as well as my eyes, and finding nothing but rough stone. Then we heard a sound from inside. We heard muffled footsteps and a key turning reluctantly in a lock, then the great door swung open creakily.

An old man in long black robes stood there, holding a silver lamp which cast long dancing shadows over the walls behind him. His face was deathly pale, almost as white as his mass of hair, but his lips were full and red and when his eyes caught the light of the lamp they bored into us almost hypnotically. He looked at Sarah and then at me. The thick eyebrows, which almost met in the middle, raised a little.

'Welcome to my house,' he said in perfect English. 'Enter freely and of your own will.'

'We were lost,' I said. 'Your driver offered us a lift but he brought us here instead of back to our village.'

The man seemed to ignore what I'd just

said. 'Come in. Come in. It is cold outside and you must be tired and hungry.' He stood back for us to enter.

The great hall had a high ceiling and block stone floor. A staircase rose from the centre and we followed the man up this, then up another flight and along a passage and into a large room with a welcoming log fire. A table was spread with food and the sight of it made my mouth water. It was ages since we'd eaten and I realised just how hungry I was.

'It's very kind of you,' said Sarah. 'Can we phone our parents? They'll be really worried.'

The man turned to look at her. 'Phone?' he said, sounding really surprised. 'I do not know that word.'

'Telephone,' said Sarah slowly, making what I thought must be an internationally understood sign. Still he frowned and shook his head. 'I do not understand,' he said, turning back to the room.

'Here is your room, young Sir,' he said to me. 'What is your name?'

'Jonathan Harker,' I said. 'And this is Sarah Western.'

His eyes opened wide. 'Jonathan Harker? How strange. I know another with your name. I have had property dealings with him. Is it a common name where you're from?'

I shrugged and he opened another door. 'Beyond is a smaller room for the young lady.' This room too had a comfortable bed and a washstand with a basin and jug of steaming water, just as mine had. It was as though we had been expected.

'I'm sure you wish to wash and then you must eat and sleep. I won't join you at your meal, I have eaten already. I will waken you at six.'

We ate roast chicken and cheese and salad because we were hungry but neither of us really enjoyed it.

'You'd think he'd have a phone, living out here,' said Sarah. 'Mum will be frantic. Do you think they're looking for us?'

'Of course they're looking for us, but they won't be looking here, will they? They'll be looking on the mountain. And how come this is all ready?' I swept my hand round the room.

'It must be a guest house,' said Sarah.

'What, without a phone?' I said. 'How do people make bookings? It's weird. And why do we have to get up at six o'clock?'

We went to bed, hoping things might look better in the morning. The man would surely get us home in the sleigh or maybe he'd send someone out to a phone.

I didn't sleep well and was up before anyone woke us. I felt about for a light switch but found only a candle and some matches. All mod cons, this place. There was already hot water in the jug and our breakfast was laid out in the other room, yet I hadn't heard anyone come in.

Sarah came in from her room holding her forehead, a pained expression on her face.

'I banged my head on the shelf in the dark. What a time to get up. Aren't there any lights in this place?' she said. 'Look, Jon, is it bleeding?'

I peered at it. 'You'll live.'

'Is there a mirror in here?'

'Yeah. I found this one in a drawer. Someone must have left it behind.'

She took the mirror, propped it on the chest of drawers behind the basin of hot water, and peered at the scratch on her face. I peered into the mirror over her shoulder and ran my fingers through my hair.

'I hope you both slept well,' said a voice behind us, making us jump.

We both turned to find the man standing there. He caught sight of Sarah's cut face and his eyes gleamed as he watched a small trickle of blood creep down her cheek and plop into the bowl of water, drop by drop, making spreading circles of pink.

His red lips parted in a smile, showing pearl-white pointed teeth.

'My dear young lady,' he said, 'you are hurt. Let me reach you a towel.' He held one out to her and I looked at his hand. The nails were cut to a point and thick, coarse hairs grew from the centre of his palms.

'It's nothing.' said Sarah. 'I shan't miss a few drops of blood.'

'I am glad to hear it,' smiled the man. 'But please try not to cut yourself. It is very dangerous. And we shall be rid of this thing,' he said, suddenly snatching up the mirror and flinging it out of the window.

'I hope the meal is to your liking,' he said, closing the window and coming back without explanation. 'I shall not join you as I have already eaten. By the way, I didn't introduce myself last night. How remiss of me. I am Count Dracula.' He bowed low.

This guy was mad. I was sure of it now. Locked up in this old castle pretending to be Dracula! Or maybe he thought he really *was* Dracula.

Sarah spun round. '*Who?*' she said. The crucifix around her neck swung wildly and I saw him stare at it and then draw back.

I spoke quickly. We must humour him. Not argue or aggravate him. We must pretend that we believed him.

'Dracula,' I said, calmly. 'You know, Sarah, you've heard the name.'

She looked at me as if I was as mad as he was. Then she glared at him. 'Look, our parents must be out of their minds with worry about us. Could your driver please take us back to Vatra now?'

'As soon as he is free,' said the man. Then he turned to me. 'I'm sure you can amuse yourselves in the meantime, can't you? There is a library along the hall.' The deathly pale face was close to mine. It was very angular and gaunt and completely colourless. His nose was long and thin, his bushy white eyebrows almost meeting above it, and his breath was so foul that I shuddered, feeling suddenly sick. It must have shown in my face, for he drew back and gestured to the table, playing again the kind host. Then he left.

I felt really uneasy and there was something else niggling my mind. Why was it that neither of us had seen him come up behind us when we had both been looking into the mirror? While he'd been looking at Sarah's cut face I'd looked into the mirror again and seen the room behind him, but nowhere could I see the man. Only Sarah and me. Where was the reflection of this man who called himself Count Dracula?

What sort of a person doesn't cast a reflection?

Chapter 3

'**H**e's mad,' said Sarah as soon as he had gone. 'We've got to get out of here. Dracula! That's that vampire story, isn't it? And you looked as though you believed him.'

'I didn't, but if we don't pretend to he might get angry.'

'What makes you an expert on madness?' She sat at the table and began to help herself to the food. 'Let's eat as much as we can and then get out.'

I sighed. She had no idea. She thought this was England. That we could just walk out of the door and we'd find a village just over the next hill. She'd forgotten how many miles we had come the night before without seeing any sign of habitation.

I went to look out of the window. It had fancy iron bars on it but peering between them I could look down into the courtyard where we had arrived last night. Behind that, the mountains were still dark silhouettes in the early dawn. Romania. I didn't know much about the country. Where was it that the Dracula story came from? Wasn't it Transylvania? I didn't know where that was – it was probably a made-up name.

I turned back to the room.

'Sarah,' I said. 'What makes a reflection in a mirror?'

She shrugged, munching on a piece of bread and reaching out for an apple. 'What's this, a science quiz?'

'That man who calls himself Dracula has no reflection,' I said.

She stopped chewing. 'Don't be daft. Everything you can see makes a reflection.'

'*He* didn't,' I said. 'We were both looking into the mirror yet we didn't see him come up behind us. He was definitely not there. I'm not imagining it. That must be why he threw the mirror away, because we might notice that he is different from other people.'

'There must be a reason,' Sarah said, sounding less sure. 'It must be something to do with candlelight. Come and eat, Jon.'

I did, and while we did so we decided we had to leave straight away. We had the whole day in front of us. I'd rather take my chances out in the snowy mountains than stay here any longer.

The landing was dimly lit with wall candles whose flickering light made dark shadows leap up and down the grey stone walls. We stepped out, closing the door quietly behind us and walked to the top of the stairs. No one. Silence. Our footsteps echoed loudly on the stone steps as we went down, for we were still wearing our ski boots. There was no sign of anyone. We had not seen anyone else since arriving here. It was strange that Count Dracula should live all alone in a great big castle. I stared up at the vast front door and then reached up and tried the handle.

It was locked.

Sarah rattled at it crossly. 'This is

madness!' she cried. 'Why are we shut in?' Her voice echoed emptily round the hall as we tried all the doors. Locked. A little tingle of fear stirred in the pit of my stomach.

There was nothing to do but go back to our room and wait for the man to return.

'Let's have a look upstairs in the other rooms,' I said.

We looked in the library but it was full of boring and very old books. Still, we had nothing else to do so we took one each and went back to our room.

The day passed slowly and we grew more and more worried about our parents searching for us. The police must have been called by now, I thought. They'd have tracker dogs out and maybe even helicopters. We ought to have something ready to wave out of the window if we heard one.

But it was getting dark now. They'd have called off the search for the day. It was the day we were due to go home – we'd missed our flight too.

'I'm going down to try the front door again,' said Sarah, standing up.

'It's nearly dark,' I said. 'What's the point?'

She didn't answer and I picked up the candle and followed her. 'We'll need this.'

Of course the door was locked. I didn't believe anyone had been near it since that morning.

'Surely you do not want to go out at this time of night?' said a voice behind us.

We both jumped and spun round. Count Dracula was standing at the foot of the stairs. His shoes had made no sound on the stone floor. He was dressed in really old-fashioned clothes: a big cape and top hat and those white things they used to wear over their shoes. He smiled, showing his sharp white teeth, and strode forward to open the great door. I tried to see what he did with the key but he was too quick.

Down in the valley wolves were howling. We shuddered and shrank back.

'What sweet music!' said the Count, listening intently. 'But you don't want to go out there. In fact, I would advise you to go back to your room now. In Castle Dracula it is wise to sleep at night.'

'We want to go back to the village,' I said. 'You can't keep us prisoner here.'

'Prisoner?' he said, raising his thick eyebrows. 'You came in of your own free will. You shall leave tomorrow.' He began to walk towards the stairs but then turned to face us again.

'I dressed up especially to show you my new clothes. I am going to London. How do I look?'

There was no answer to that. Pretty stupid, I thought. Not what you'd call cool and trendy. But let him find out for himself.

He didn't wait for an answer. 'I can't wait to get to London again,' he said. 'To mingle with the crowds.' He smiled to himself. 'How is the old Queen?'

The question took me by surprise. I'd never thought of her as old before but come to think of it, I supposed she must be.

'You mean the Queen Mother?' said Sarah, taking my advice and humouring him.

'Queen mother?' he asked, surprised. 'I mean the Queen. Queen Victoria.'

'Queen Victoria?' we chorused. He wasn't only out of date with his clothes. Where had he been?

'It's Queen Elizabeth now,' said Sarah. 'Queen Victoria's been dead for years.'

'She's dead?' he asked. 'Oh, I hadn't heard. But what other news? I was there last year to see the opening of the Tower Bridge and I was astonished to see the new horse-less carriages.'

'Horse-less carriages?' we chorused again. We looked at each other and I could see by the growing horror in Sarah's eyes that she was beginning to think the same as me.

'What year is this?' I asked him.

'You ask me the year? We may be a little backward here but we have the same year as you. It is 1895 of course. But now, I have enjoyed chatting to you but I have things to do.' He turned and went upstairs.

'Is he mad or . . .' began Sarah.

'Or have we gone back in time?' I finished for her.

'It would explain the candles and the

strange way he looked at you when you asked for the phone.'

'But then . . .' Sarah began again. 'Who are we? We haven't been born yet – and neither have our parents.'

'Look,' I said. 'If we have gone back in time it must be possible to get back to our own time again. Maybe it happened in that fog.'

'Low cloud,' she said, and despite it all, we smiled at each other for the first time.

We went back to our room, our heads whirling with the idea that out there was the world of more than a hundred years ago – or was it? It was all very confusing.

Then we heard a sound outside the door. Someone was speaking softly and another answered. Then a breathy giggle. The door handle turned slowly and the door began to open. There was more whispering and giggling when suddenly a harsh voice cut it short and the door was slammed shut.

'Not yet!' hissed the voice which we now knew well. 'Get away from here! Wait until tomorrow.'

I flung open the door and looked outside into the corridor but there was no one there.

'There are other people here,' I said. 'I'm going to find them. Let's look in these other rooms.'

Sarah was looking really scared but she followed me without speaking. The first door we tried was locked, and the second, but the third opened and we went in. A yellow shaft of moonlight poured in through the window and I ran to look out. This room faced a different direction from ours. As far as we could see were mountains, high and jagged and gleaming white with snow. I pushed open the heavy window and heaved myself on to the broad windowsill for a better look. Far below were forests, a winding river. I looked down. What I saw then almost made me fall back into the room with fear.

The castle was built on the side of an immense precipice. Anything falling from this window would fall hundreds of feet without touching anything.

'What's the matter?' asked Sarah, staring out.

'Have a look down there.'

We both peered through the open window. The night was cold and the stars were out. We were staring down the steep walls of the castle when something suddenly moved. Someone was climbing slowly out of a window directly below. First his head emerged and then the rest of his body. His dark billowing cape spread out like wings. And then he began to crawl head first down the castle wall like some gigantic and horrible bat.

Chapter 4

We both slowly backed away from the window as if at any moment the floor might crumble under our feet and send us hurtling into that awful emptiness.

We looked at each other. I could see the whites of Sarah's eyes in the moonlight.

'What is he?' she whispered.

I had no answer. We went back to our room and shut the door.

During the night I thought I heard the sound of digging far below and noises in the courtyard woke me the next morning. Voices seemed to be shouting instructions in a strange language and now and again a horse whinnied and hooves clattered on the cobbles. The snow must be melting.

I jumped out of bed and ran to the window. Some large boxes were being brought out and loaded onto a wagon.

The door opened and Sarah came in. 'Are you up, Jon? There are people outside. We can ask them to take us back to Vatra.'

I didn't ask her how, when they most likely wouldn't speak English and when we couldn't get out to speak to them anyway. We went over to the window and opened it. We tried yelling and waving things out of the window but none of them even looked up. They were too busy with their work.

'What are those boxes?' asked Sarah. I don't know why she asks questions like that. How am I supposed to know? At one time I would have made some sarcastic answer but we were both in trouble and there was no use having arguments as well.

'Dunno. They look heavy.' The thought crossed my mind that they looked like coffins. At one time, too, I would have made a joke about them being Dracula's victims but somehow I couldn't say the words, though I knew it was all stupid.

'We've got to get that key,' I said. 'He must keep it in his room.'

Sarah looked at me. 'We know where that is. It's the room he came out of last night.'

'Before crawling headfirst down the wall,' I said, watching her face, testing to see whether what I'd seen the night before was true or just my imagination. Dad says I have a vivid imagination. Maybe it *had* been a bat after all. Maybe they had some huge species there.

It wasn't a bat. Because Sarah nodded. She didn't argue or laugh. She nodded. She'd seen him too.

'Let's try now,' I said. 'He never seems to be around during the day.'

We went downstairs and looked for the appropriate door. It was locked. We should have known.

'There's only one way, then,' I said. 'Out of the window.'

Sarah looked aghast. 'Don't be silly, Jon. How can we do that?'

'Have you never heard of tying bedsheets together to make a rope? That is what we'll do. And I'm the lightest. I'll go.' I heard myself saying those words as if I were volunteering to abseil down the wall of the school gym. But this was for real. I thought of that terrible precipice and my mouth went dry. 'We have to escape. You heard him say he's going to London.'

'And leaving us prisoners,' said Sarah slowly. 'What did he mean when he said to those laughing people "not yet, wait until tomorrow"?'

'I really don't know,' I said. 'Except that tomorrow is now today.'

Together we set to work on the sheets and the curtains, making strong knots and a sort of harness. When it was ready we carried it to the other room and unfastened the window.

I dared not look out. I knew what was there. Nothing. A sheer castle wall and a cliff face dropping away hundreds of feet into a ravine. Certain death if the makeshift rope did not hold. Had anyone ever really tried one or was it only in adventure stories?

My hands shook as I got into the harness. My heart pounded so much that I felt dizzy.

The other end of the rope was attached to an iron bedstead which we had dragged nearer to the window. Then Sarah wound a loop around her waist ready to pay it out, and turned to me. The moment had come. She put her arms round me and I let her. Then I climbed onto the windowsill and put one foot tentatively outside.

The wall of the castle was not quite as smooth as it looked. Over the centuries the wind and rain had eroded the mortar from between the large stones providing small hand- and footholds.

Don't look down, I told myself. The stones were rough and cold beneath my fingers. The harness chafed at my ribs painfully and I tried to put more weight on my feet to relieve the tension as Sarah slowly let out the rope. A slight breeze buffeted me and threatened to dislodge me. On and on I went, trying not to think of where I was, just that this was our only chance.

Something horrible waited for us in the castle, I knew that.

Then I felt the top of the Count's window with my toe. I was there but what if the Count was in his room, watching my every move, waiting for me to get level before he . . .

The window was open a crack and I clutched at it and pushed it up. The room was empty. As I swung myself inside I gave Sarah a wave.

As soon as I had let her in, we quickly began our search for the key but it was obvious that it was not there. There was very little in the room, just a chair and a table and one or two small cupboards. Strangely, no bed. But there *was* another door, smaller than the main one.

'Let's try that door,' I said when we'd looked in the cupboards.

It opened easily as if much used. Beyond it a flight of winding stone steps led downwards, lit only by an occasional wall candle. The air smelt damp and stale and reminded me of Dracula's breath.

'We need a candle,' said Sarah, looking round the room but finding none. 'I'll go back to our room and get one.'

She was soon back and together we went down the steps, Sarah holding the candle aloft. At the bottom of the steps was a short passageway which led to a room. There were no windows and I thought that we must be underground in a cellar. The stone walls were greenish and glistened damply in the flickering light. I shivered as we looked round. A couple of boxes still waited to be loaded onto the wagons, half full of what looked like ordinary earth. That would explain the digging sounds I'd heard. Their lids lay nearby waiting to be fitted. Another box, set apart from the rest, was against the far wall. Its lid was loosely laid on top and several nails were already partly hammered in, just waiting for the final fixing.

'Nothing much down here,' whispered Sarah. 'I wonder what all these boxes of soil are for.'

'Growing tomatoes?' I suggested with a nervous giggle. I hadn't yet recovered from my ordeal down the castle wall and I was still shaking.

Sarah was not amused.

'We could hide in the boxes until the men load them onto the wagons,' I said.

'They nail them down,' she said.

For a moment I thought it would still be worth a try but then I thought again. No, it wouldn't.

I don't know what made Sarah go over to the box by the far wall, maybe just natural curiosity because it was closed, but I knew what would be inside, and I told her so.

'It'll only be soil, like the rest,' I began, but she was already giving me the candle. 'Hold this for me,' she said. 'High, so we can see inside.'

She began lifting the lid slowly and laid it back against the wall. I raised the candle.

The sight filled my soul with such horror that I almost dropped it.

Chapter 5

Inside the box on a layer of earth lay Dracula, but not as we had ever seen him. He looked young again: his white hair was dark and his cheeks were full and rosy instead of deathly white. From the corner of his mouth a trickle of dark red blood had run down his chin and onto his neck. His whole face looked bloated like someone who has just gorged himself on a huge meal and his eyes were open though he did not appear to be breathing and there was no sign of life.

I backed away a little and the candle flame wavered, distorting the horrible face into even more hideous expressions. Dracula did not move but it seemed to me that his eyes watched us and his mouth smiled mockingly.

Then, with a shock, I knew the awful truth. I'd read about vampires, haven't we all? Horror stories that give you shivers down the spine, but which you know are nothing but legend or superstition.

But this wasn't fantasy. It was real.

The way he cast no reflection, was never seen during the day nor ever ate with us. His ability to walk down sheer walls like a bat. His sharp pointed teeth, the hairs on his palms and now his young and bloated appearance. And the blood. The blood around his mouth. He didn't eat like normal mortals, did he? Count Dracula was a vampire. One who fed on blood. Whose very existence depended on it. And those he fed upon also became vampires, the Undead, preying on yet more victims.

And Count Dracula was soon to be on his way to London where, perhaps for centuries to come, he would create an ever-widening circle of monsters to prey upon the population.

Sarah reached out her shaking hands and lowered the lid and just then came the sound of someone coming in, more than one person, for we could hear voices. I blew out the candle and we hid behind a large pillar, watching as two men took up a hammer and securely nailed the lid onto the box in which Dracula lay. Then they lifted it up and carried it away and we followed.

At the far end of the cellar was a small door through which we could see daylight but as soon as the men were through, someone shut it behind them.

'We've got to get out that way too,' I whispered. We made our way towards the door, keeping well to the sides of the cellar in the shadows. As we reached it we heard the crack of a whip, then a creaking noise as the wooden wheels began to move.

'What about the other boxes?' I whispered but Sarah had her hand on the door.

It was locked. She cursed and I raised my eyebrows in mock surprise, though she couldn't see me. There was a crack about a centimetre wide in the slats of the door and we both peered through. The wagon was just disappearing from view.

From behind us in the darkness of the cellar the murmur of voices reached our ears, an echoing peel of laughter, high and breathy.

I jumped and my foot kicked against something. I bent to pick it up. It was one of the hammers the men had used to nail the lid onto the box. And it was the sort with a hammering end and a flat end. I wedged the flat end into the gap in the door and levered at the slat with all my strength.

Behind us the whispering got louder. Sarah grasped the slat of wood and we both worked on it. At last, with a splintering sound, it broke away, making a hole just large enough for us to squeeze through.

When we were outside we ran to find our skis. They were still lying where the coachman had flung them, only now the snow had almost melted, revealing cobblestones. We just picked them up and ran as best we could in our ski boots until we were well away from the castle and into snow again.

'Don't worry,' I said. 'They can't come after us while it's still daylight.'

Sarah didn't question it. She had obviously read about vampires too.

We skied all day. At least, some of the time we skied and some of the time we side-stepped uphill, one weary foot after another. As night fell the wolves began howling again and the wind rose, blowing the clouds across the moon. We couldn't see anything in the pitch black.

We rested for a while in the hollow of a small hill, huddled together for warmth, and even slept a bit. At one time I thought I heard that same stifled giggling and whispering and Sarah did too because she grabbed my arm so tightly that she nearly stopped the circulation, but I didn't say anything. Then we set off again and when at dawn the sun glowed hazily through the mist, it found us trudging uphill again, into a thicker fog. My skis felt like lead weights. We were too exhausted to speak. On and on we went, unable to see further than a couple of metres in front of us.

After a while the fog cleared a bit and we were surprised to see that the sun was really low in the west. The day had gone faster than we thought.

I squinted ahead. Then I stopped.

'Sarah! Look! A chairlift!' And I knew we were safe. Back in our own time.

We took off our skis outside our chalet and clattered into the porch in our boots. Dad opened the door.

'Have a good day?' was all he said.

Sarah's mum was pouring a cup of tea and she looked up with a smile as we came in. 'I said you'd probably ski down,' she said. 'You wouldn't let a bit of fog put you off on your last day.'

So it was the same day! Time had gone much more slowly here. We must have looked stunned because Dad said, 'Are you all right?'

I nodded and bent to unclip my ski boots. I pulled my feet out of them and waggled my toes. It felt good.

'Can fog have a funny effect on you?' I asked.

'How do you mean?' asked Dad.

'Well, can it make you imagine things?'

'It can certainly make you disoriented,' he said. 'So that you don't know where you are. Even familiar places can seem strange, and especially here, with the white snow as well. Why? Did you get lost and stray off piste?'

'Yes,' I said. 'We did stray off piste.'

Sarah's mum put a hot cup of tea in front of me. 'Never mind,' she said, 'you're back safe and sound.'

'We're back,' said Sarah, and lifted her cup to her lips.

Chapter 6

I closed the front door and threw my school bag down onto the hall floor. It was still strange coming to this house instead of our old one, where I'd lived all my life. At least I hadn't had to change schools. Mum still lived in our old house, close enough for me to visit when I wanted, but it wasn't the same. I'd liked my old room with the window looking out over the bit of back lawn and the wilderness Mrs Oxford called her garden. Now it had a new view over a great dilapidated house the Council was probably going to knock down. Good thing, too. What a monstrosity!

Sarah and her mum were still moving things from their flat. Their rent was paid up until the end of the month so they were taking their time. She and Dad had married just before our skiing holiday. I suppose that was their honeymoon.

My stomach rumbled noisily so I went to see what was in the fridge. I was just reaching for a wedge of left-over pork pie and the orange juice carton when something soft brushed against my legs. I jumped. The piece of pie skated dangerously around the plate and the orange juice splurged out onto the floor.

A small black cat stood looking up at me and it opened its mouth and mewed.

'That's Sooty,' said Sarah from the doorway.

'How original,' I said. 'Who thought of that name?'

Sarah ignored my sarcasm. 'Can you be careful when you open the door, Jon? She musn't be let out for a few days, until she's used to living here.'

'Her and me both,' I muttered. 'You didn't tell me you had a cat. Where was she during our holiday?'

'Our old neighbours looked after her.'

It was the first time we'd mentioned the holiday since we'd got back two days earlier. It seemed silly now to mention what had happened to us in the fog, let alone the name Dracula. I did look up Transylvania though and found it was a region of Rumania in the Carpathian mountains, which is where we were. Funny that. And I went to the library to borrow the book *Dracula* by Bram Stoker. It was out on loan.

Sarah perched on a kitchen unit. 'What do you think happened in Rumania?' she asked. She must have been reading my mind.

I shrugged, biting into the pie. 'It must have been the fog, like Dad said. Disorientation. Or maybe the cold. That can have a funny effect on you. It was just a sort of hallucination.'

'How do you explain this then?' she said.

I looked up. She was holding up something attached to a chain round her neck. It was the crucifix the person had ...

'You must have found it in the snow,' I said, quickly.

'No, I didn't,' she insisted. 'You remember

that person threw it into the sleigh. And I lost my ski badge too.'

I ignored the first thing she'd said. 'They're only cheap, those ski badges, or they wouldn't give them to everyone. I'm not surprised it fell off.'

She ignored my jibe. 'Who's going to clean up that spilt orange juice?'

'Not me,' I said, slamming the fridge door. 'It was your cat which caused it.'

Nothing had changed. I resented her. I did not want a stepsister or a stepmother. I wanted my own mum back. Ok, so they'd been separated for a few months, but living at Gran's had seemed sort of temporary. There'd always been the chance they would get together again, until Dad had met Sarah's mum. Even then I'd hoped it just wouldn't last. But now they were married.

I went out of the room so Sarah wouldn't see the tears in my eyes.

'I didn't think you liked cats,' I said to Dad later that evening when we were alone.

He grinned. 'I don't,' he said, 'but it seems a nice little thing.'

It just shows, doesn't it? I bet if I'd wanted a cat it would have been a different story.

'Talking of animals,' said Dad, 'some dog jumped off a ship last night when it docked. They're warning people not to touch any strange dogs in case of rabies and to report any sightings to the police.'

I laughed. 'That should keep them busy.' Dad laughed too as we thought about how silly that was and it was a bit like old times.

'Tell Sarah about it too, will you?' said Dad. 'Since she's potty about animals.'

Saturday was Sarah's mum's birthday and we were celebrating it by going for a meal and a show in the West End on the Friday night as Dad thought it would be easier to get tickets. Sarah's mum said she didn't mind what show we went to and we could choose.

'*Cats*,' said Sarah without giving me a chance. I might have known she'd choose that. My distaste must have shown in my face because Sarah's mum said: 'It depends what we can get tickets for, but have a think about it.'

Well, I wasn't going to give in without a fight. 'I'd rather see *Starlight Express*,' I said.

Dad phoned up. 'I can get tickets for both,' he said, putting his hand over the phone, 'what's it to be?'

In the end we tossed for it and she won. *Cats* it was. Actually I enjoyed it but I tried not to show it.

We went by bus as it's useless trying to get a parking space. On the way home we sat up top, me next to Dad with Sarah and her mum in the seat in front. We were going along Piccadilly towards Hyde Park Corner and had stopped to let passengers on and off when a figure suddenly caught my eye and my heart gave a lurch. It couldn't be! It was impossible! I leaned forward, poked Sarah's shoulder and pointed.

He was standing under a street lamp by the railings of Green Park just watching the people go by. He couldn't have been more than three metres from our bus. He was tall and thin and well-dressed, not in the old-fashioned clothes he'd shown us in

Transylvania, but in a suit and shirt and tie, with one of those expensive beige-coloured coats around his shoulders. He had a beaky nose and a black pointy beard. His lips were full and red and his mouth was open in a half smile, showing very white teeth. He looked young, just as we'd last seen him in that box of earth leaving the castle.

I still had my fingers on Sarah's shoulder and I felt her stiffen. Then she turned in her seat and looked at me, her eyes wide with horror.

'He's here!' she whispered. 'Mingling with the crowds of London.'

'But that was . . .' I began. That was 1895. Was he here again? In our time? Why not?

'Who is it?' asked Dad, looking past me.

'Just someone we thought we recognised,' I said.

When we got home I went to Sarah's room.

'What's happening?' I asked. 'Was it true, what happened to us in Rumania? It was definitely him, wasn't it? What can we do? We ought to tell someone.' For once it was me making silly suggestions but she didn't mock me. We both knew that no one would listen.

'Could we say he kept us prisoner and threatened us?' asked Sarah. 'No, because we were never missing. The time that we were in the castle passed much more quickly than present day time.'

'But why did it happen to *us*?' I asked. 'There must be a reason.'

'We ought to find out about vampires,' said Sarah.

'I have.'

'You have? You didn't tell me.'

I reached for my encyclopaedia. Had she forgotten? We hadn't been speaking to each other. There was a bookmark in the page. I laid the book on the floor and she peered over my shoulder. I hate people doing that.

'I have read vampire stories before,' I said, 'but I never took that much notice.' I positioned myself so that she couldn't see the page very well and began to read.

'The legendary Transylvanian vampire is said to be a trapped soul inhabiting a body neither alive nor dead. It is commonly called the Undead and it is recognisable by its gaunt appearance and deathly pale skin. Its lips are full and red and its canine teeth are sharp and pointed. With these it pierces the jugular vein of its victims and drinks their blood. It has eyebrows which meet in the middle and coarse hairs growing on the palms of its hands. Its breath is foul.

'A vampire's remarkable strength is derived from its diet of blood and it has the ability to control the weather and to change into other forms, often that of a wolf or bat.

'By day it must rest in its own grave or in earth from its grave, for the rays of the sun are fatal to it. Another sure means of destruction is said to be a wooden stake through the heart. Garlic and crucifixes are also powerful deterrents. The victims of vampires will ultimately become vampires themselves.'

I sat back on my heels and looked round at Sarah. She was practically as pale as a vampire herself and she just stared back at me.

At last she said, 'But it's not a legend, is it? It's true.'

'I suppose all legends are partly true,' I said. 'That's how they start in the first place.'

'But this isn't partly true, it's totally true! Every word of that was what we saw.'

I said nothing.

'Wasn't it?' she insisted.

I nodded. If it was some sort of dream, how could we both have had the same one? Crazy at it seemed it must be true. And we'd just seen him, that night, in Piccadilly. Back in London again. What could we do?

My mind was filled with the problem all the next day, which is probably how I came to leave the back door open so that Sooty escaped. Sarah was so angry and worried, she was almost crying.

'She'll be all right,' I said. 'She's lived here for a week.'

'But it's nearly dark!' she shouted, flashing me an angry look and dashing out after the cat. I followed. Sooty's black tail was just disappearing through the hedge into the overgrown garden of the old house next door. We had to run round to the front and in through the gate and by that time the cat was nowhere to be seen.

Sarah looked at me despairingly and for the first time I felt sorry that I hadn't been more careful. We strode around through the long grass and bushes, towards the house itself.

'Sooty!' called Sarah, pushing aside the thick foliage.

Then we saw her, or at least her tail, vanishing into the ground.

Near the wall of the house a big iron trapdoor was set into the ground like the ones outside pubs for delivering beer barrels. Next to the trapdoor the earth had given way so that there was a space and that's where Sooty had gone. I could see where Sarah got her curiosity from now. They say owners get like their pets.

Sarah bent down and tried frantically to lift the metal door but it wouldn't budge.

'She'll get out again when she's hungry,' I said casually.

I think she could have hit me then. 'Who asked you?' she yelled. 'You don't care! I love Sooty! She's part of my life! I don't need you!'

Funny, I'd never considered what she felt about me. She must resent me just as much as I did her. And Sooty was a link with her old life. I grabbed the handle of the trapdoor and helped her pull.

At first nothing happened. Then I noticed the thin layer of soil and dust on top of the door shuddering a bit. The door was moving but it felt as if it were locked from below. We stopped for a moment to get our breath back and in the silence came an echoing meow from the hole. Sarah began pulling again with renewed strength, more panic really. The door moved a bit more and then opened so suddenly that we both fell over backwards.

We looked down into the gaping hole. No glowing cat's eyes greeted us.

'Sooty!' Sarah called again.

'It must be the cellar,' I said. 'There are some steps. Let's go down.'

'Be careful. They're probably rotten.'

I let myself down, holding the door surround and not putting my full weight on the steps until I was sure they would hold me. It wasn't far to the bottom. Only about two and a half metres. I blinked in the darkness and looked round as Sarah followed. There wasn't much in the cellar and it wasn't very big. An old wooden box stood against one wall and on top of it sat Sooty, calmly washing a front paw.

Sarah took her in her arms, murmuring in her ear and stroking her head.

'What does that remind you of?' I asked, indicating the box.

Sarah looked at it. 'That one is old and falling apart,' she said. 'The others were made of new wood.'

I was about to point out that the ones we were speaking about were more than a hundred years old when she thrust Sooty into my arms and bent down to lift the lid. She was at it again. She couldn't go by a box without opening it to see what was inside. The lid opened easily. This one wasn't nailed down. I held my breath as she lifted the dusty wood, remembering the last time.

But there was no body in this one. Nothing much at all really. It was very dirty inside and the wood was crumbling.

'What's that?' exclaimed Sarah and leaned in to pick up something off the bottom.

I don't know how it happened, but the next thing she'd fallen right inside and the lid had slammed shut on top of her. I sighed with exasperation and put Sooty down so I could use both hands to lift it again.

The box was empty.

Chapter 7

It was impossible! Someone can't just disappear. It was like some awful conjuring trick. Perhaps if I closed the lid and opened it again she would have reappeared.

I tried it.

She hadn't.

I looked round the cellar. She was not hiding in a corner, nor had she gone back up the steps, but I went to look, just to be sure. When my head had reached ground level I looked about.

'Sarah?' No reply. Just a meow from Sooty, who had gone up the steps and was sitting on the grass a few feet away. She knew where her home was all right.

I went back down into the cellar and

opened the box again. What had Sarah been looking at? There was nothing in the box except a few inches of dirt.

So I did what she had done. I climbed in and closed the lid after me.

There was no sensation of falling or whizzing through space. I had no sooner closed the lid and opened it again when I knew something was different. Sarah was standing in the cellar looking at me and holding something in her hand. The cellar was newer than before and the box I climbed out of was new too, exactly like the ones in Dracula's castle.

'It's happened again,' said Sarah. 'I'm sure it has, though I haven't been outside yet. I was waiting for you to come.'

'We've gone back in time?'

She nodded and held out her hand to show me what was in it. It was her ski badge.

'That's what was in the box,' she said. 'That's what I saw and reached in for.'

'How could it have got there?' I asked. There I was again, asking stupid questions which she couldn't answer.

We walked towards the steps which led outside. They were newer and so was the trapdoor.

'It's dark,' she said. 'But there's a moon.'

The garden was not much different from the one we'd left though the grass was shorter. The house itself was in much better condition. We walked towards the hedge, *our* hedge, and looked over. Sarah gasped.

Our house was basically the same although the windows were different and there was no conservatory on the back. The garden was completely different. There were a lot more bushes and a bird bath in the middle of a circular lawn. There was also a long garden seat and on it lay Sarah's mum. But that wasn't what had made her gasp. It was the fact that someone was leaning over her. Someone in a long black cape. As if he felt our gaze on him, he looked up and his pale face shone white in the moonlight, the shadows accentuating its gauntness. His eyes gleamed red and his thick lips were parted in a smile.

'Mum!' There was agony in Sarah's voice as she sped round to the front, through the gate and into our garden. I was only a second behind her.

The dark figure had gone. And it was not Sarah's mum, we could see that now, although she looked quite like her. This woman looked pale and she seemed to be unconscious. We didn't know what to do.

'Let's see if there is anyone else in the house,' I said.

'You go, I'll stay with her,' said Sarah.

I went and knocked on the door and it was ages before I saw a glow in one of the windows and then heard someone coming downstairs. I had no idea what the time was here.

The door opened and a man stood there in his night clothes holding a candle. He looked me up and down and I realised how strange I must look in jeans and T-shirt.

'There's a lady,' I began. 'She's not well.' I waved my hand behind me. The man looked past me, saw her and then dashed out, almost knocking me over.

'Lucy!' he cried. 'Oh, my darling Lucy!'

The woman had come round now and was trying to stand up with Sarah's help.

'We're from next door,' I said, trying feebly to explain our presence in the middle of the night. 'We're from a hundred years from now' would have sounded a bit far-fetched.

But he wasn't listening. He had his arm round Lucy and was half carrying her towards the house. At the last minute he turned his head and said to us, 'You'd better come in.'

The house was very different inside. In the kitchen was a wooden table and chairs and he sat her on one of these while he reached into a cupboard for a bottle of golden liquid which I guessed was brandy, and poured her a drop in a cup. He'd put the candle on the table and now he turned to a lamp on the wall which made a hissing sound until he lit it with a match. Gas lights, I thought.

We could all see each other better now and the woman seemed to be recovering. She raised her head and gave us a weak smile. Was it a trick of the gaslight or were her canine teeth slightly longer than normal? I shuddered. She looked like a nice person. She had really deep blue eyes and a friendly face. I must be wrong. The door opened and another man came in and looked round at us all.

'What has happened, Jonathan?' he asked. I blinked as he said my name. Then I realised he was talking to the other man.

'Lucy was walking in her sleep again,' said the man called Jonathan. 'I am very worried, she looks so pale.'

'There was someone with her.' Sarah spoke for the first time and both men looked at her sharply.

'These children are from next door, Jack,' said Jonathan. So he had heard after all. He looked at Sarah. 'What was the person like? The one you saw with her?'

Sarah looked at me and I knew what she was thinking. How far should she go?

'He was thin and very pale,' she said. 'He was wearing a dark cape.'

The two men looked at one another. Then

Jack came forward to bend over Lucy. She didn't seem to be aware of him. Gently he pulled down the collar of her nightdress and peered at her neck. He blanched.

'The marks are there again,' he said, 'fresher than ever.'

'We know the man,' I said, knowing that I was risking ridicule. 'His name is Count Dracula and he comes from Transylvania. He's a . . .' I hesitated to say the word.

'A vampire,' said Jack, nodding. 'We know, and he roams London in search of unsuspecting victims while no one listens to us.'

I know the feeling, I thought.

'We must get Lucy back to bed now, Jonathan,' he continued, helping her to her feet. She seemed still to be in a daze and stood up like a zombie. 'Make sure she wears the garland of garlic flowers around her neck and spread more about her room. We must do everything we can to deter this evil monster.'

He turned to us. 'Meanwhile, I thank you,' he said. 'Go back safely to your beds.'

We left and went back to the house next

door and the cellar. As we climbed down through the hole I looked up. On the branch of a nearby tree a bat hung, upside down. Its brown eyes glinted in the moonlight and there was something familiar about them.

Chapter 8

We climbed out of the earth box and were in our own time again. It seemed that this was a means of travelling through time, like the Tardis, except that Doctor Who never knew where he would end up, or *when* I should say. We, I supposed, would always go back to 1895, if, that is, we ever wanted to go back.

As we went through the gate I noticed an old wooden sign and stopped to squint at it in the semi-darkness.

'What is it?' asked Sarah, coming back to look.

'The house name, I think. I can only make out CAR . . . the rest is too faded.'

Sooty was sitting on our back doorstep waiting to go in.

'You were right,' said Sarah. 'She knows where her home is.' Suddenly she grabbed my arm. 'Jon!'

'What?'

'That dog!'

'Which dog?' Honestly, I can't follow the way her mind works sometimes.

'You told me a dog jumped off a ship.'

My heart lurched. Dog, wolf. Now I had it. 'You think it might have been him?'

Sarah nodded.

'One thing's for certain,' I said, opening the back door, 'if we ever go back into that earth box, we'd better go at night. It might be occupied during the day.' Personally, I couldn't think why we should want to.

At least we were talking to each other now. She wasn't so bad really. We didn't talk much about Dracula, though. I suppose she, like me, felt slightly guilty that we weren't doing anything about warning people, but how could we? I didn't think *Crimewatch* would take us seriously. Imagine explaining the photofit bits. Face? *Thin and very pale*. Teeth? *Very white with a sharp pointed one on either side.* Eyebrows? *Bushy and meet in the middle.* Distinguishing features? *Hairs on his palms. Long, pointed fingernails. He may even be in the form of a wolf or bat.* The public are warned to keep away from this man and to report sightings to the police. He is suspected of . . . what? Being a vampire?

It was exciting too. Scary, but exciting. We knew something that no one else knew. It was that secret which sort of brought us together.

I went to see my mum nearly every day after school. She only spoke about our holiday once, just after we'd got back. There she was, in our old house as usual, giving me a Coke and a piece of cake when I came in. Just like before – except that mostly I didn't stay, I went back to my new home. She was still doing her old job, running a playgroup in the mornings. Once or twice I nearly talked about Sarah but then I stopped just in time. I didn't suppose she'd want to hear about Sarah.

When I got back from Mum's Sarah was

always very quiet as if she knew I was afraid to tell my mum about her and was offended. I dunno. Whatever you do you upset someone.

A couple of nights later a horrible noise outside woke me up. I got out of bed and looked out of the window but of course I couldn't see anything. It was a howling, yelping sort of noise, like an animal in pain. I heard someone in the passage and opened the door. It was Dad.

'Woke you too, did it?' he said, crossly. 'Wretched animal.' I followed him downstairs and he picked up a torch, opened the back door and shone the beam around.

Silence. Nothing moved.

'Typical!' he said.

The howling started again and he stepped outside in his slippers.

'Dad!' I whispered urgently.

He turned back and looked at me questioningly.

'Be careful.'

'It's only a dog,' he said.

Only a dog. Was it?

I felt someone come up behind me. It was Sarah. She was clasping the crucifix in her hand.

'He should have taken this.'

'Don't be daft,' I said.

Just then we both saw a dark shape run across the lawn and disappear into the hedge between us and the old house.

'Get out!' we heard Dad yell and the torch beam wavered wildly as he shook his fist at it.

'It might be that dog off the ship, Dad,' I said when he came in again.

'I'll phone the RSPCA tomorrow,' he said. 'Off to bed, you two.'

The RSPCA inspector did a thorough search of the house but found nothing.

'Except a bat in the loft,' he said.

Sarah and I looked at each other.

'What have you done with it?' asked Sarah.

'Done with it?' he asked. 'Bats are protected. It's illegal to move them or destroy them. They're harmless.'

Not this one, I thought.

There was another sign of Dracula's presence, though again only Sarah and I recognised it. The local television news said that a number of people had gone down with a strange illness in which they suffered from sudden shock and had to be rushed to hospital for emergency transfusions. The illness caused mental confusion and nightmares and the appearance of two red marks on the neck. So far cases were confined to the London area and patients were being isolated in case the disease was infectious. The cause was unknown and there was no obvious link between sufferers.

There was an article in the *Evening Standard* too.

'I'm going to phone them up,' I said to Sarah as we gazed down at the headline.

'So what are you going to say?'

I ignored her. I was already punching out the number I had found on the back page.

'Evening Standard.'

'Could I . . .' I began, searching my brain for the right phrase. 'Could I speak to someone about the illness?'

'Illness?' said the male voice at the other end. 'What illness? Who are you?'

'You know, when people need a blood transfusion.'

'I'll put you through to the news desk.'

My hand was sweating and my heart thumping. I passed the phone over to the other hand.

'News desk.'

'It's about that illness,' I began again.

'I'm listening,' said the new voice.

I decided to go for it. Sarah was sighing in exasperation at my side. I nearly handed the phone to her.

'Doesn't it remind you of anything?' I asked. 'Two marks on the neck, loss of blood?'

'They thought at first it was some tropical snake,' said the reporter, 'until they had several cases and knew that one snake couldn't get around that fast. What are you getting at? How old are you?'

'You're not going to believe me, but . . .'

Sarah gave me a sharp nudge.

'We know, my . . . stepsister and me, that

vampires are true and . . .' There was a loud guffaw of laughter.

'Vampires!' the reporter said. 'Now why didn't I think of that? Two marks on the neck, loss of blood.' I could hear laughter in the background too. 'You've given me a good idea though, son, we can call it the *vampire syndrome* until someone comes up with a diagnosis.'

He put the phone down, still laughing. I felt sick with humiliation.

'Why didn't you . . .' began Sarah.

'Why didn't *you* make the phone call?' I yelled in her face, and rushed out of the room, slamming the door.

Next day there were two more cases of the illness. The headline read 'Two More Fall Victim to Vampire Syndrome'. They didn't realise just how true that was.

I went back to the library and this time they had the Dracula book. The front cover was a still from a really old film with some actor called Bela Lugosi playing the part of Dracula. It didn't look a bit like the real Dracula. You could tell he had lipstick on.

Three hundred and seventy-eight pages of really small print – and this was a condensed version. It would take ages to read. I flicked through the pages until something caught my eye. Two words jumped out at me and I staggered back as if they'd hit me in the face.

Jonathan Harker.

My name. Also the name of the bloke in the book.

I slammed the book shut and put it in my school bag. I couldn't open it again until I was at home with Sarah.

'Weird!' she said, when I told her. 'Let's have a look.'

I pulled it out of my bag and gave it to her. She glanced at the cover and then opened it, methodically scanning the pages, not flicking through as I had. Then she stopped and looked up. Her face was pale.

'It's the same,' she said. 'The castle bit. Jonathan Harker is kept prisoner there and left to the other vampires but he escapes. Dracula leaves for London by ship, bringing boxes of earth with him. He lands in Whitby. Where's that?'

'Yorkshire. My mum's got a friend there.'

Sarah leafed through the book again. 'His first victim is called Lucy and . . . she dies.'

I looked at her. Lucy was the name of the lady from the past who we'd found in our garden with Dracula bending over her.

'We must go back. We must see whether she's all right,' I said. 'The book must be a true story and for some reason we keep living it. It's one step on from virtual reality. It's total reality.'

Sarah nodded slowly, her eyes staring at me in a glazed way. IIer hands were shaking.

'There's something you haven't thought of, Jon,' she said.

'What?'

'My mother's name is Lucy too.'

Chapter 9

We decided to go that night, after sunset, anyway. And since present time seemed to stand still while we were in the past, we didn't even bother to say we were going anywhere to Dad and Sarah's mum.

We climbed down the steps into the cellar and I shone the torch on to the old wooden box.

'I hope he's not still in there,' said Sarah.

'It's after sunset,' I said.

'He could be having a lie in,' she giggled, nervously.

I laughed too and it echoed round the small cellar. The laughter somehow eased the tension.

We opened the lid.

It was empty except for the soil. Sarah got in first and closed the lid. Then I opened it and got in, very aware that this was soil from Dracula's grave. I shuddered. Not long ago *he* had lain here. I hoped vampirism wasn't catching – not in this way, anyway.

Soon I was climbing out of the box and Sarah was there waiting. Together we climbed up the steps and through the trap-door.

Next door in our house, or Lucy and Jonathan and Jack's as it was then, there was only a faint glimmer from the kitchen window.

'Shall we go and knock on the door?' asked Sarah. 'Say we've come to ask after Lucy?'

We walked round and through their front gate and were just going down the side of the house when we heard the front door open. There was the sound of voices. Something made me pull Sarah into the bushes and as we watched, Jack and Jonathan came out, closed the door, and walked up the path right by us. Jonathan seemed to be holding back, as if reluctant to go wherever it was they were going. I almost stepped out to speak to them then but realised it might give them a fright and they'd wonder what we were doing lurking in their garden at whatever time of night it was.

Jack was carrying a bag from which he took something out and held it up to show Jonathan. 'The key to Lucy's tomb,' he said. 'There's something we have to do, Jonathan.'

I heard Sarah gasp beside me. 'She's dead.'

It was a shock, but not a surprise. It had to happen, didn't it? This was the story which the book told. Our story was the one which was happening in our time. History repeating itself.

We followed the two men out into the night, keeping a distance between us. It was fine and quite warm. The moon was almost full so we could see where we were going. The streets were almost deserted. I really wanted to look about me although the road wasn't that much different except for having gas lamps instead of electric ones. There

the key. Then with a creak, the heavy wooden door opened to reveal a dark interior. After a little hesitation, the two men stepped inside.

I crept forward to the doorway, followed by Sarah.

A new coffin stood inside on a stone plinth. Flowers hung lank and dead around it and the brass plate gleamed dully in the lamplight as Jack took out a tool from his bag and began to work on the coffin lid, removing the screws, I guessed.

With a groan, the heavy lid was raised. I felt Sarah's fingers dig into my arm but she stayed where she was.

We both heard Jonathan's cry of horror.

'It's empty!' he said.

'Are you satisfied now, Jonathan?' asked Jack.

'Perhaps it is the work of a body snatcher,' said Jonathan.

Jack shook his head. 'So you need more proof? Come with me.' He put the lid back on the coffin and Sarah and I ran back into the shadows as the two men came out of the tomb again. Jack locked the door and put the key in his pocket.

'Now we wait,' he said. 'I shall take up position on the far side of the cemetery while you watch from behind that yew tree over there.'

Sarah and I moved further away from the tomb and tried to make ourselves comfortable on a grassy hillock behind another gravestone. Then we waited as the church clock struck two, then three. Sometime later my eyelids were drooping when Sarah suddenly nudged me.

'What's that?' she whispered.

Something white was moving between the gravestones on the far side of the churchyard beyond the scattered juniper trees by the gate. A darker shadow followed it and I thought it must be Jack. Somewhere a cock crowed and a cloud passed across the moon but there was already the brightening of dawn in the east so it was not completely dark. Someone appeared almost in front of us, carrying something in his arms. Then another figure appeared.

'You see. Now do you believe me?' said a voice which I recognised as Jack's. 'It's a child. We were just in time. And look. The same marks on her neck. We must find a policeman to take her to hospital, and then return. The deed must be done immediately.'

'It was a child,' whispered Sarah when they had gone. 'It's awful. How could she?'

A cock crowed again and made us jump. Then something caught my eye, something white, coming towards us through the gravestones and the trees. A figure in white, her features clear in the moonlight. Lucy, the lady we'd helped, who looked like Sarah's mum. But how she had changed. The gentleness which had been there had turned to cruelty. Her lips were red with fresh blood which trickled down her chin and stained her white gown.

I shuddered with horror but could not move, as if fixed to the spot. Sarah did not scream but I wouldn't have been surprised if she had. This was not the Lucy we had met briefly, only a creature with her form and colouring. The eyes which had once been a deep gentle blue now blazed with hell-fire. But she still somehow resembled Sarah's mum. She saw us and smiled, ice cold and full of venom. Then she reached out her arms to us.

'Come to me,' she said.

It was then that Sarah screamed and I thrust something in front of the creature's face. She gave a cry and stepped back, shielding her eyes, then ran towards the door of the tomb. Then, as we watched in horrified amazement, her body which had looked so solid seemed to dissolve and pass through the crack of the door where hardly a knife blade could have gone.

Then Jack and Jonathan appeared, striding up the path underneath the lightening sky.

'What are you doing here?' asked Jack.

Sarah had gained some control of herself and it was she who spoke. She pointed to me.

'He is Jonathan Harker, too,' she said. 'And my mother's name is Lucy. We are from the future and it is all happening again in our time. Dracula is back.'

They looked at us and I could see that they were having difficulty believing us. Well, who wouldn't?

'Go back,' said the other Jonathan. 'Go back to your own time. We shall deal with him. Never fear, we shall not let him escape.'

'It will not be so easy,' said Jack. 'Dracula is more cunning than a mortal man for he has had much time to learn it over the centuries. He can command the weather and grow or become small. He can change into any form he wishes and sometimes even vanish altogether. It is a very dangerous thing we are trying to do and if we fail – he wins.'

'We shan't fail,' said Jonathan with conviction.

'And Lucy?' I asked. 'She is back in the tomb.'

They both looked towards the tomb, then Jack nodded and set off, Jonathan following.

We didn't do as they suggested and go back. Something drew us to the tomb too and Jonathan lit the lamp while Jack took a sharp wooden stake and a hammer from his bag. Then he looked up.

'This is not the Lucy whom you knew,' he said to Jonathan. 'This is not my dear sister and your beloved wife. She is now a vampire, one of the Undead, who cannot die but must go on age after age acquiring new victims. We must help her to rest as true dead so that the soul of the poor lady whom we both loved shall again be free to take her place with the other angels in the kingdom of God.'

He lifted the stake and the hammer.

We averted our eyes while the deed was done. When we heard a blood-curdling scream we turned back to look. The thing in the coffin shook and twisted in wild contortions and the sharp white teeth clamped together. Then it was still. Gradually the real Lucy took its place, her face sweet and gentle and peaceful.

'And now,' said Jack to Jonathan, 'you may kiss her as you couldn't before. She is no longer the Devil's Undead, but God's true dead. Her soul is with Him.'

Jonathan bent and kissed her and then Jack lowered the lid of the coffin and screwed it down. We all left the tomb, locking the door behind us. Outside the air was sweet, the birds sang and the sun was about to break over the horizon.

Suddenly I grasped Sarah's arm. 'Run!' I yelled. 'We have to get back to the box before dawn.'

She looked at me in horror and we both set off at a sprint, raising a hand to the two surprised men as we sped through the cemetery towards the gates and the road home.

If we didn't make it in time, something else would be occupying the box.

Chapter 10

I reached the box first and heaved up the lid. It was still empty! With no thought for Sarah I dived in and shut it and when I got out I was in our own time again. I stared back at the box guiltily. Oh well, I thought, if Sarah were trapped there it would be for only a day. As soon as night fell she could come back.

The lid opened and she leapt out, gasping for breath.

'Thanks a lot!' she panted. 'Talk about saving your own skin!'

I looked suitably shamefaced.

'And how come you had the crucifix too?'

'I saw it on your dressing table just before we left. I thought we might need it so I picked it up and put it in my pocket. I meant to tell you.'

'Yeah, yeah,' said Sarah. 'What if I'd got in the box and then *he*'d got in?' She shuddered.

'Well he didn't,' I said. 'We're back safely and we never need to go back again. Lucy is dead and we have to trust Jonathan and Jack to find Dracula and destroy him.'

'Well they obviously didn't, did they?' she said.

I stared at her.

'If they had got him he wouldn't be back now.'

It was confusing. 'Unless us going back somehow changed the past,' I said.

Sarah was silent for a moment as we made our way back to our house. 'But we didn't really *do* anything,' she said.

It was true. We had done nothing to change history. We went back to bed. In the morning Sarah's eyes were red and puffy and she looked as if she had hardly slept. As I came into the kitchen she was holding out the crucifix to her mum.

'Sarah, I don't want it. Not to wear anyway. Where did you get it?'

'Someone in Rumania gave it to me,' said Sarah.

'Well you keep it,' said her mum. 'I quite like crosses on chains but I don't want to wear a crucifix.'

Sarah flashed me a look of desperation. She was so afraid for her mum but how could we warn her? Because her name was Lucy we thought Dracula might strike? Because history was repeating itself? He killed Lucy and then who? What happened next? I hadn't read the book. Who killed him in the end?

My heart lurched. Wouldn't the hero of the book be the one to kill him? The hero was Jonathan Harker.

I was Jonathan Harker. Was I going to have to do what Jack had done to Lucy? I shuddered. No way.

'Hurry up with your breakfast, you two,' said Sarah's mum. 'This is a weekday. You haven't got time to mess about.'

I got home just after Sarah that afternoon because there were no after-school activities.

'I tried to get some garlic flowers,' she wailed. 'But the florist didn't know what I was talking about so I went to the supermarket. They only had garlic bulbs.' She held up two strings of them. 'Do you think they will do?'

I shrugged. 'Yeah, why not? It's garlic. What are you going to do with it? I don't suppose your mum will wear it round her neck any more than she would the crucifix.'

I saw her lip tremble and realised I'd sounded as if I didn't care. 'Put them in her room,' I suggested. 'And the crucifix too. It's at night that she's in danger.'

I went with her to Dad's and Sarah's mum's room and she hung one string of garlic over the headboard of the bed hidden behind the pillows and the other at the end of the curtain rail. Then she looked round for somewhere to put the crucifix.

'Over the door,' I suggested, though why Dracula should use the door or the window when he could presumably seep through a crack, I didn't know. But she did what I said.

When we were back in my room she said,

brightly, 'He might even have gone, mightn't he?'

I didn't want to heap on the worry but I couldn't let her think that. 'Sarah, we did nothing to change history but maybe we can find out what went wrong.' I reached for the Dracula book and turned to the back. Then I read and reread the final pages.

'I've got it!' I said. 'You remember Jack said that vampires have to have a wooden stake driven through their heart?'

She nodded.

'Well, they didn't do that to Dracula. They did it with a knife. A metal knife.'

She frowned. 'Why?'

I looked back at the book. 'They were in a hurry. Night was falling. Look, here it is on page three hundred and seventy-six. "The Count was lying within the box upon the earth. His eyes glared with hate, but then he saw the sinking sun and the look turned to triumph."' I looked up at Sarah. 'So Jonathan quickly killed him with a knife. A *metal* knife.'

'We've got to go back then,' said Sarah.

'And tell them where they went wrong.'

We couldn't wait for the evening, for sunset, when we could go and warn Jack and Jonathan. The days were getting quite long now as summer drew nearer. Sunset wasn't until about half past eight. Dad phoned to say that he was going to be late home so we went ahead and had tea and we had just finished when Sooty flew in through the cat flap like a rocket, her tail all fluffed up to about twice normal size.

Sarah's mum went outside to see what had frightened her and we heard her talking to someone – or something. She was talking in that sing-song sort of voice people use for babies and animals.

We went to look.

It was dusk but we could make out a shape by the shed. It was a dog. A medium-sized dog, quite thin with scruffy brown and white fur. It stood poised ready to run. Mum bent down and held out her hand.

'No, Mum!' shouted Sarah. 'Don't go near it!' Her mum ignored her. I could see for the first time that she was soppy about dogs.

'It might be that dog off the ship,' I said. 'It might have rabies.'

The dog was getting brave and some of the fear had gone out of its eyes. Its thin tail came out from between its legs and began to wag a little uncertainly. Then it took a few steps forward.

'Mum! Leave it!' I could see that Sarah was getting desperate. So was I, and it wasn't rabies we were worried about.

Just then there was a polite cough behind us and we all turned at once. A man had come unnoticed up the side of the house. He was dressed in a suit like Dad wears to work only this one was real smart. His hair was short and perfectly in place – in fact he looked like he'd just stepped out of some posh men's shop in London. His face was thin and bony and he had a small pointy beard.

It was Dracula.

Chapter 11

'**G**ood evening,' he said. 'I do hope I didn't startle you.'

'Oh no,' said Sarah's mum, straightening up. 'Can I help you?'

'I hate to intrude,' said Dracula, 'but I was just having a look at the house next door. Carfax. I used to live there long ago and I am considering buying it again and renovating it.'

'That would be nice,' said Mum. 'It is a bit run down.'

'Indeed,' said Dracula. 'So you see, we may be neighbours, so I was anxious to meet you.'

He turned to look at Sarah and me with

those hypnotic eyes and he frowned a little as if trying to think where he'd seen us before.

'What charming children you have.' He smiled showing those white teeth. It was too dark to see the pointy ones but I knew they were there.

'Can I offer you a cup of tea?' asked Sarah's mum, turning towards the back door, having forgotten about the dog, which, incidentally, had disappeared.

'You're so kind,' said Dracula, his voice as smooth as silk, 'but I have a dinner appointment and I shall be dining soon.'

If only she knew, I thought, if only Sarah's mum knew just what he would be dining on. A very boring diet of BLOOD. Another victim tonight would get those two puncture marks on their neck. I wondered who it would be.

'I'm Lucy Harker,' said Sarah's mum. 'And this is my daughter Sarah and my stepson Jonathan.'

Dracula turned to me, a strange look in his eyes. 'Jonathan Harker,' he said slowly.

Then his face relaxed into a smile. 'I hope we meet again,' he said with a small bow towards Sarah's mum. He turned on his heel and left as quietly as he had come. We knew all about his silent approaches, Sarah and I. And another thing we knew too. That dog was not him. That was a relief.

'What a charming man,' breathed Sarah's mum. She was staring after him as if mesmerised. 'What wonderful old-fashioned manners.'

'He does seem very old-fashioned,' said Sarah, looking at me, 'but I don't think I'd want him as a neighbour.'

That was the understatement of the century!

'Oh but I'm sure he would be a very nice neighbour,' said her mum. 'But funny, he never introduced himself.'

I wasn't surprised.

'You shouldn't judge people by their looks,' said Sarah.

'That's true to some extent,' said her mum, ' but I'm sure you *can* tell a lot from a person's appearance.'

Not this time, I thought. And *she* would have to be very careful with him around. I wondered about going to buy some more garlic and even a crucifix or two. Where did you buy crucifixes? Tomorrow I'd find out. I could go and ask the priest at St Benedict's Catholic Church in Ramborne Road. Maybe vampires could be exorcised like ghosts. That was a thought.

As it happened, all our efforts were for nothing. My dad found the garlic. One of his cufflinks had fallen between the bedside table and the bed and he'd been rummaging down the side for it.

He came into the the living room holding the string of garlic at arm's length, wrinkling up his nose. I couldn't smell anything.

'What's this, Lucy?' he asked Sarah's mum.

'Garlic,' said Sarah.

He turned to her. 'I know it's garlic, but what's it doing hanging on the headboard of our bed?'

Sarah's mum looked at us. Then, without saying anything, she went out of the room and came back a few minutes later with the other string of garlic and the crucifix.

'What *is* this?' she sighed. 'What's going on with you two? First you want me to wear a crucifix round my neck and now this. Is it to ward off evil spirits or something? Do you have some crazy idea that this house is haunted?'

'Yes,' said Sarah with a rush, jumping at this suggestion. 'We think there's an evil spirit nearby.'

Dad snorted with laughter and I gave him a look of disgust. I couldn't even rely on him to back us up, or at least to listen seriously. If we'd said we thought we could smell a gas leak he'd have turned the house upside down to find it before it caused trouble, but mention evil spirits, never mind vampires, and he was all scorn.

'You two have been watching too much TV,' he said.

Typical. I'd heard that before. About a million times.

'Please, Mum,' said Sarah. 'Put it back where it was, just to please us. Just for one night.'

'I will not. Smelly stuff.' Sarah's mum turned and went out. 'I'm never going to be able to use all this garlic. What a waste. You kids have got more money than sense.'

We went to bed not knowing what else we could do.

Later I woke up and felt a cold draught on my face. I opened my eyes. Maybe I should close the window. As I tried to decide whether or not to get out of my warm bed, the curtains began to billow out and a strange mist poured in, slipping under and between the curtains. The mist became thicker and thicker and formed a column above my bed. Then from out of the mist came a face, which bent over me, closer and closer, until I could smell that foul breath. The red mouth opened and the white, razor-sharp teeth reached towards my neck. His red eyes held mine and I couldn't do anything. I wanted to scream, to jump up, but I felt paralysed. I couldn't drag my eyes away from his. Then I felt a heavy pressure on my neck.

Chapter 12

At last I was able to move. I got up quickly and the room seemed to turn upside down. I felt sick so I lay down again for a minute and then tried again, but more slowly. My legs felt like jelly as I tottered to the door and went to Sarah's room.

'What is it?' She blinked in the sudden light and sat up.

'He was here,' I whispered. My voice shook. 'He came in like a mist through my window. I saw his teeth and then ... Look! Please look at my neck, Sarah.' I bent down and Sarah squinted at my neck. Then her hand flew to her mouth and she fell back on to the pillows.

'They're there, aren't they?' I whispered. 'The two red marks.' I felt suddenly very weak and dropped down on to her bed.

'What am I going to do?' Tears sprang into my eyes. Dracula had attacked me. Would I die now and turn into a vampire? I was in mortal danger but I couldn't even tell my dad or my mum. I really wanted my mum.

'Why you?' asked Sarah.

'He knows my name,' I said. 'Your mum introduced us this afternoon. It was a Jonathan Harker who tried to destroy him last time so he's afraid of me. He's making sure he gets rid of me before I get him.'

Sarah was silent. She reached out and put her arm round my shoulder and I let her. It felt good.

'We've got to go back,' she said. 'There's still a chance we can warn Jack and Jonathan that he must be destroyed with a wooden stake and not a knife. Maybe we can still change history. Come on. Get some clothes on.'

I still felt a bit dizzy but better than before. I went back to my room and dragged on my jeans and jersey. Then we crept downstairs and out of the back door. I pressed the button to illuminate my watch. Half past one.

There was no sign of Dracula in any shape or form in the garden. Not that we could see much anyhow. Sarah had the torch and we went round to the front gate. The street lights glowed reassuringly until we were in the blackness of Carfax's garden. I took some deep breaths of fresh night air and felt better, except that I was scared silly.

One by one we climbed into the earth box and went back to 1895.

The house where Lucy lived was all in darkness, which you would expect in the middle of the night. We went round to knock on the back door and it was then that we saw the note. It was attached to the door with a small nail and the ink had run a bit as if it had got wet in the rain.

'Hold the torch up,' I said to Sarah, hoping we could still read it. 'It must be for us.'

Dear Jonathan and Sarah, I read, *Our*

enemy has fled back to his own country and we are in pursuit. Never fear. We shall destroy him. Signed – Jack Western and Jonathan Harker.

Sarah and I looked at each other.

'We're too late,' she whispered.

I felt a cold fear creep over me and the dizziness came back, so I sat down on the doorstep, my head in my hands.

'What are we going to do?' I felt sick. I was going to die. Then I would become a vampire and prey on people for the rest of eternity. And Sarah's mum was still in danger too. But I was the one who posed most threat to Dracula. Why hadn't I thought of it? At least I could have had some of the garlic.

I felt Sarah tugging at my arm. 'Are you all right, Jon? Let's go back. We're too late here. We have to destroy him in our own time.'

I knew it was true but still the idea didn't appeal to me very much. I'd seen what they did to Lucy's vampire.

We went back round to the cellar and

climbed down the steps. Then Sarah screamed.

The whole place was alive with rats.

They swarmed all over the floor and over the earth box and over each other. Hundreds of them. We ran back up the steps. I took the torch from Sarah and my hand shook as I shone it down into that boiling mass of dark bodies. Their eyes glittered like a thousand tiny lights.

'It's him,' I said. 'It's him, trying to stop us from getting back to our own time. If he traps us here in 1895 he can escape.'

Sarah was gripping my arm so tightly it was beginning to go numb. I could hear her gasping breath as she tried to stifle another scream.

As we watched, the rats kept on multiplying until they were two or three deep and the sound of their horrible squealing echoed round the cellar.

One or two had begun leaping on to the steps. 'Shut the door!' screamed Sarah. 'Don't let them out!'

I heaved the door shut and we stood

there, in the darkness of Carfax garden, wondering what we were going to do. We were trapped in the nineteenth century.

Chapter 13

'**I** wish your Sooty were here,' I said, going to sit on a garden seat where we could still watch the trapdoor for signs of escaping rats.

'Sooty!' exclaimed Sarah. 'They'd eat her alive. That stray dog would be better.'

'That's it!' I jumped up. 'A dog! If we could find a dog and bring it back here . . .'

Sarah looked at me. 'It would have to be a big fierce dog to frighten that lot, and how can we make it come back with us?'

I tried to think. 'Look, this is London in 1895. There are probably lots of very hungry stray dogs around.' I looked across towards the house next door. 'I'm sure Jack and Jonathan wouldn't mind if we broke in to find some food to lure a dog.'

It was good to be doing something. We ran round next door and easily forced the window open. We found a tin of corned beef and an old fashioned tin opener and I wrote a note for Jack and Jonathan explaining what we'd done. Then we set off to look for a dog.

They say that a dog's sense of smell is a hundred times greater than ours and I believe it. We'd hardly gone up the road a few metres when two dogs came skulking out of an alleyway and followed us at a distance. One was a small, dirty, long-haired animal and the other a battered black dog which looked as though it had seen a few fights. Soon another one joined us.

'I feel like the Pied Piper,' I said.

Sarah was in no mood for jokes. 'Won't these two do?' she asked. I could see she was getting apprehensive. These were hungry dogs and could attack us at any moment.

'Yeah, let's get back.'

There were five dogs with us by the time we got back to the cellar.

'We'll chuck the meat down into the cellar,' I said. 'I reckon they're so hungry they won't even see the rats.'

Cautiously I lifted the trapdoor. For a moment those rats swarming up the steps drew back at the torchlight, but then they surged forward and poured out all over my feet and on to the lawn in a great black flood. Sarah screamed again and ran to stand on the seat. I wanted to do that too but I stood my ground, my stomach turning over as I watched one or two try to climb up my legs.

The dogs too seemed a little afraid at first. I expect that rat meat was about all they ever ate, but never this much at once. I held the tin under their noses and then tipped out the chunk of corned beef into my hand and threw it down into the cellar.

Three of the dogs dived down after it, scrambling over the mass of rats in a frenzy of hunger.

The rats were afraid too. The ones which were outside were being chased by the two remaining dogs while the ones just coming up the steps turned and ran back down again.

'I think they're going,' I said.

Sarah cautiously got down off the seat and came to look, watching where she put her feet. Sure enough the mass was becoming thinner until just a few scurried here and there, chased by the dogs who had, by now, eaten the corned beef.

'Jack and Jonathan said Dracula was going back to his own country,' said Sarah. 'His power must be getting weaker as he gets further away. It was a good idea about the dogs, Jon.'

I grinned as we climbed down and went towards the box. 'Thanks, dogs,' I said.

'Pity we can't get them any more food,' said Sarah. 'Poor things.'

'You're as bad as your mum,' I said, opening the lid of the earth box for her to get in first this time, but I felt sorry for them too.

We went back to bed. I grabbed the garlic as we went through the kitchen, tied the two strings together, and hung my makeshift necklace round my neck. There was a faint smell but I didn't care. I shut the window too. We had to wait until daylight and get Dracula while he was in his earth box. Then we'd decide what we had to do. I was not looking forward to it.

Chapter 14

I didn't feel any different the next day, not weak or dizzy any more, I mean. I bared my teeth in front of the bathroom mirror but they looked the same as usual, the two front ones a bit crooked and no sign of the side ones getting longer or pointier.

School dragged. I couldn't wait for half past three yet I dreaded it too. Three times Mrs Andrews told me off for staring out of the window instead of getting on with my work. One day I'll tell her how important it was for me to think. One day when the world realises that there are such things as vampires. That is, if I'm not one myself by then. Now there's a thought. If I was a vampire I could *show* Mrs Andrews, couldn't I?

At twenty-nine minutes past three I had an idea. At half past I was through the door and heading home as fast as I could.

'Sarah!' I burst through the door, scaring Sooty out of her wits.

'She's gone to see her dad,' said her mum. 'You're home early, Jon.'

Her dad! How could she, today of all days! I'd practically forgotten she had a dad.

'He's back in England. He phoned to ask if she could go round as he hasn't seen her since our holiday,' continued her mum.

That's right. I remembered now. Sarah's dad was away a lot, on business. He always had been. I bet she missed him. For the first time I realised that it was the same for her. Her family had been split too. She probably hadn't wanted a stepparent and a stepbrother or stepsister any more than I had.

'She'll be back about eight o'clock,' her mum went on. I nodded and went upstairs. It would be nearly dark by then. My plan would have to wait until the next day. Saturday. It *must* be sunny weather.

Sarah arrived home about a quarter past eight.

'How is your dad?' I asked.

'OK.' She shrugged, and then turned away. I was right. She didn't want me butting in. She didn't want me at all. She wanted her dad and her mum. Together. But it could never be. I knew just how she felt and I left her alone.

That night I wore my garlic necklace again.

In the morning Sarah was her usual self again. I told her my plan. We had to destroy Dracula.

'This is the easiest way,' I said. 'I don't fancy the stake through the heart routine.'

Sarah shuddered. 'Are you sure this will work, Jon?'

'According to the book it will,' I said. It *had* to work.

We went round to Carfax after breakfast the next morning and opened the trapdoor. Sarah stared at the box.

'He's in there,' she whispered. 'Do we have to open the lid?'

'Of course we do,' I said, not feeling as brave as I sounded. 'But we have to judge when the sun's rays will be shining directly down through the hole. It's still shadowed by the house at the moment. We have to drag the box out so that it's underneath the opening.'

That was my plan. Sunlight was fatal to vampires. We would drag out the box and then open it and expose him to the sun. Even as I thought about it I felt a brisk wind on my cheek. I looked up. Huge billowing black clouds were gathering on the horizon. There was a roll of thunder.

'He knows,' I said. 'We have to be quick.'

We went down the steps. Every step I took felt like walking further and further into a trap. I could feel his presence there, just a few metres away. I wanted to turn and run, to slam that door behind us and never come back. But we couldn't. We had to do this.

The wind was brisk now and a flash of lightning split the sky. We ran to the box.

It was really heavy and had been in that place for over a century so that it had almost taken root. We each took an end and pulled and tugged. It didn't move. Outside the wind howled and above it I thought I heard Sarah's mum calling. That's all we needed, for her to come looking for us.

Sarah looked at me and I knew she'd heard her mum too. We both hesitated, not knowing what to do. I glanced back at the trapdoor opening. The sky looked black.

'Go and see what she wants,' I said. 'I'll look for something to slide under this box. I'm sure once we get it moving it'll be easier.'

She ran up the steps and disappeared. I looked round the small cellar. There was nothing much there. Just the box. I was aware all the time of Dracula's presence, as if he were emitting some sort of radiation. It filled the cellar, almost overwhelming me.

I heard Sarah coming back and at that moment found what I was looking for. An old fire poker.

'The sky's nearly clouded over,' she said.

I jammed the poker under the box and levered it up. Did the box move a fraction? I pushed again. This time it went under a little further.

'I think it's moving,' I whispered. I tried again. The box creaked and shifted a little and we looked at each other in triumph.

Once we got it going it was a bit easier but dragging with your back bent is tiring work. But it was moving. Little by little. I glanced up at the trapdoor opening.

'It's getting dark out there,' I said. 'We have to hurry!'

The wind had really whipped up and a few twigs and leaves blew in through the opening as we positioned the box underneath. The black cloud had reached the sun and was beginning to cover it . . .

Frantically, we both got hold of the lid and heaved.

It fell open and crashed to the floor behind and my heart lurched. Dracula lay inside. His eyes were open and he glared at us for a moment before turning them to the sky. I looked up too. For an instant it looked as though we were too late, then the cloud parted and a last burst of sunshine came through the opening. I looked back at Dracula. His face seemed to soften and relax. He looked at us again with a different expression now. A kind look. A grateful look. His trapped soul had been released, free to rest in peace at last. Then his body dissolved into a cloud of dust which settled on to the earth in the box.

He was gone. We had won.

For weeks I peered into the mirror for signs of growing teeth and examined my palms minutely for any hair growth, but there was none. I suppose one attack wasn't enough.

Lucy persuaded my dad to let us keep the stray dog. Our Lucy, I'm talking about. My stepmum. Because the dog came back and we knew it was safe.

Carfax is being demolished and they're going to build four houses on the site. The bulldozers started work yesterday. You can't even see the cellar door any more, it's covered with rubble.

For a while Sarah and I both felt we wanted to tell someone about Dracula but we knew it was no use – they wouldn't listen, and now it all seems like a dream.

Anyway, Jonathan Harker saved the day again, didn't he?

But the earth box is still there, buried under the ground, waiting . . .

Author's Note

The idea for Dracula came to its author, Bram Stoker, in a nightmare, after which he began research in Whitby Library reading about a very nasty fifteenth-century king called Vlad the Impaler (son of the dragon) who used to impale his enemies on stakes.

It was in the British Museum that Bram Stoker continued researching the legends of vampires which began in south-eastern Europe more than two thousand years ago.

THIS VOUCHER ENTITLES YOU TO 2 FOR 1 ENTRY TO:

Ride the nightmare! Take a boat trip on 'Judgement Day – Sentenced to Death'. It's a one-way journey to meet your maker in this terrifying recreation of 18th Century 'justice'.

Catch the plague at the York Dungeon! Take a spine-tingling tour around the plague-ravaged streets of 14th Century York in the company of your grisly guides.

The London Dungeon, Tooley Street, near London Bridge tube station. Telephone: 0171 403 7221 for further information and opening times.

The York Dungeon, 12 Clifford Street, York. Telephone: 01904 632599 for further information and opening times.

Terms and Conditions
1. This voucher will admit one adult or one child free to the London or York Dungeon when accompanied by an adult paying the single day adult admission.
2. This offer is not valid in conjunction with any other offer, promotion or voucher.
3. A child is classified as aged 4–14 years inclusive. Under 4's are admitted for free.
4. There is no cash alternative to this offer.
5. Photocopies of the voucher will not be accepted.
6. This offer is valid until 31 December 2000.